TALES FROM CHINA

OUTLAWS of the MARSH

Vol. **02**

OUTLAWS of the MARSH

Vol. 02

Thick As Thieves

Created by WEI DONG CHEN

*Wei Dong Chen is a highly acclaimed artist and an influential leader
in the "New Chinese Cartoon" trend. He is the founder of Creator World,
the largest comics studio in China. His spirited and energetic work has attracted
many students to his tutelage. He has published more than 300 cartoons in
several countries and gained both recognition and admirers across Asia, Europe,
and the USA. Mr. Chen's work is serialized in several publications,
and he continues to explore new dimensions of the graphic medium.*

Illustrated by XIAO LONG LIANG

*Xiao Long Liang is considered one of Wei Dong Chen's greatest students.
One of the most highly regarded cartoonists in China today, Xiao Long's
fantastic technique and expression of Chinese culture have won him
the acclaim of cartoon lovers throughout China.*

Original Story
"The Water Margin" *by Shi, Nai An*

Editing & Designing
Mybloomy, Jonathan Evans, KH Lee, YK Kim,
HJ Lee, JS Kim, Lampin, Qing Shao, Xiao Nan Li, Ke Hu

Characters

Volume 02

ZHISHEN LU

ZhiShen Lu, also known as Major Da Lu, is a respected and feared former military official. But the only thing more dangerous than his brute strength is his impulsive behavior, behavior that lands him on the wrong side of the law and hiding in monasteries to avoid a murder charge. But despite his violent nature, ZhiShen Lu can't help but become a protector to those who can't protect themselves.

ZHONG LI

Zhong Li is a bandit who lives on Peach Blossom Mountain. While Zhong Li and his partner are known to cause trouble in the region, he becomes an unexpected peacekeeper when ZhiShen Lu gets involved in his affairs.

DAOCHENG CUI

DaoCheng Cui, who calls himself Iron Buddha, took control of WaGuan Temple by force and uses his power to torment and kill the priests of the temple and force himself on the women of a nearby town. But when an unlikely liberator arrives at the temple door, DaoCheng Cui knows he must prepare for a fight.

CHONG LIN

Chong Lin is a marshal of the Imperial Guard who befriends ZhiShen Lu, but then runs afoul of YaNei Gao, the treacherous son of Grand Marshal Qiu Gao. Despite his years of dedicated service, Chong Lin is forced into exile, and learns there is no limit to the depth of Qiu Gao's treachery.

Characters

YANEI GAO

YaNei Gao is the adopted son of Qiu Gao. He has done nothing in his life to earn the power he wields, and he uses the power largely to force women to do his bidding. So when YaNei Gao takes a liking to Chong Lin's wife, infatuation soon turns into a matter of life and death.

QIAN LU

Qian Lu is a childhood friend of Chong Lin, and even serves under him in the Imperial Guard. But fidelity means nothing to Qian Lu when he's offered a bribe, and no childhood friend will come between him and a few bars of gold.

DING SUN

Ding Sun is an official in the court of KeiFeng, where Chong Lin is put on trial for a crime he didn't commit. Despite Qiu Gao's desire to have Chong Lin killed, Ding Sun convinced the court to spare his life and send him into exile.

QIU GAO

Qiu Gao is the treacherous Grand Marshal of the Imperial Guard, and probably the most powerful man in the Song Dynasty. Raised in poverty and destitution, Qiu Gao rose through the ranks and achieved his position through a combination of cunning, flattery, and scheming.

Chapter 1

When ZhiShen Met Chong

Summary

Tong Zhao has made an enemy of ZhiShen Lu when he forces Lord Liu's daughter to marry him. When ZhiShen Lu humiliates him in front of Liu's family and his own men, Tong Zhao retreats to his mountain base and asks his fellow bandit, Zhong Li, to avenge him. But Zhong Li is familiar with ZhiShen Lu, and the conflict is soon resolved.

ZhiShen Lu continues to make his way toward DongJing, where the monks of WaGuan Temple put him in charge of running a farm on the outskirts of their land. ZhiShen is even less of a farmer than he is a monk, but he wins the loyalty of the farmhands and, during a demonstration of his martial arts skills, the admiration of a soldier named Chong Lin.

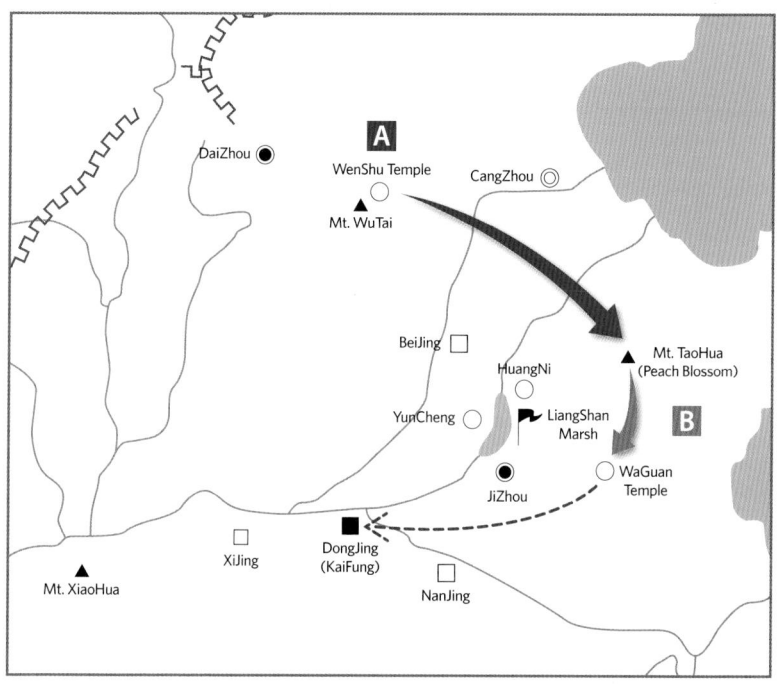

A Wanted for murder, Da Lu, with the help of Lord Zhao, disguised himself as a Buddhist monk and hid himself at WenShu Temple.

B Da Lu, renamed ZhiShen Lu, does not adapt well to monastic life, so he is sent by Elder ZhiZhen to another temple in DongJing. Along the way, he makes a fateful stop near Peach Blossom Mountain.

11

13

I BELIEVE YOU ARE A SOLDIER. BUT YOU MUST NOT LEAVE US TO HIM!

DON'T WORRY. I'LL FINISH THE BANDITS ONCE AND FOR ALL.

Meanwhile, Tong Zhou ha[s] retreated to h[is] mountain bas[e] where he told [his] master, Zhon[g] Li, what had happened. Zh[ong] Li was incense[d] at the news, a[nd] offered to ave[nge] his partner.

HE'S RIGHT. OUR LIVES ARE IN YOUR HANDS.

WHERE IS THIS MONK NOW? I'LL GO STRAIGHT THERE AND BREAK HIM OVER MY KNEE!

THMP THMP THMP THMP

15

IT'S NOT WHAT YOU THINK, MY LORD.

FORGIVE ME. I DIDN'T MEAN TO SCARE YOU BEFORE.

WHA...? I'M SO CONFUSED.

WHAT'S GOING ON? ZHISHEN, WHY HAVE YOU BROUGHT THE BANDIT INSIDE?!

AFTER I FLED WEIZHOU, I HOLED UP FOR A TIME IN DAIZHOU, AFTER WHICH I WENT TO LIVE IN A MONASTERY. WELL, YOU CAN IMAGINE HOW WELL THAT WENT OVER! HA HA!

OH, DEAR...

SIGH.

THE ELDER OF THE TEMPLE HAD NO CHOICE BUT TO SEND ME TO ANOTHER TEMPLE, WHICH IS WHERE I WAS HEADED WHEN I STOPPED HERE.

WE'RE ALL DEAD NOW.

23

Thanks to ZhiShen Lu's intervention, the dispute over the marriage was settled without incident.

MAJOR, I'D LIKE TO INVITE YOU TO OUR MOUNTAIN BASE. YOU COULD STAY FOR A FEW DAYS.

FINE BY ME. LORD LIU, WHAT DO YOU SAY?

OF COURSE!

THE NEXT EVENING...

WHAT IS GOING ON HERE? THIS MONK HUMILIATES ME, BUT INSTEAD OF AVENGING ME, YOU MAKE HIM OUR GUEST?

HERE'S TO NOT HOLDING ANY GRUDGES IN THE MORNING.

AFTER ALL, A GOOD NIGHT'S SLEEP IS HEALTHY. WHETHER BY DRINK OR CONCUSSION.

BAM

SHUMP

AND THANKS FOR THE TABLEWARE. MOST KIND OF YOU.

BETTER STAY OFF THE MAIN TRAILS.

THERE'S ALMOST NO CHANCE I'D AVOID RUNNING INTO MY TWO FRIENDS.

31

WAGUAN TEMPLE

HOW DID IT FALL INTO RUIN LIKE THIS? DOES NO ONE LIVE HERE?

ANOTHER TEMPLE. ALTHOUGH THIS ONE LOOKS AWFUL.

HELLO! ANYONE HOME? SPARE SOME CHARITY FOR A TRAVELING MONK?

SHOONK

KREEK

HEY, YOU THREE! WHAT ARE YOU DOING IN HERE? AND DIDN'T YOU HEAR ME?

WE HEARD YOU. STOP SHOUTING, ALREADY.

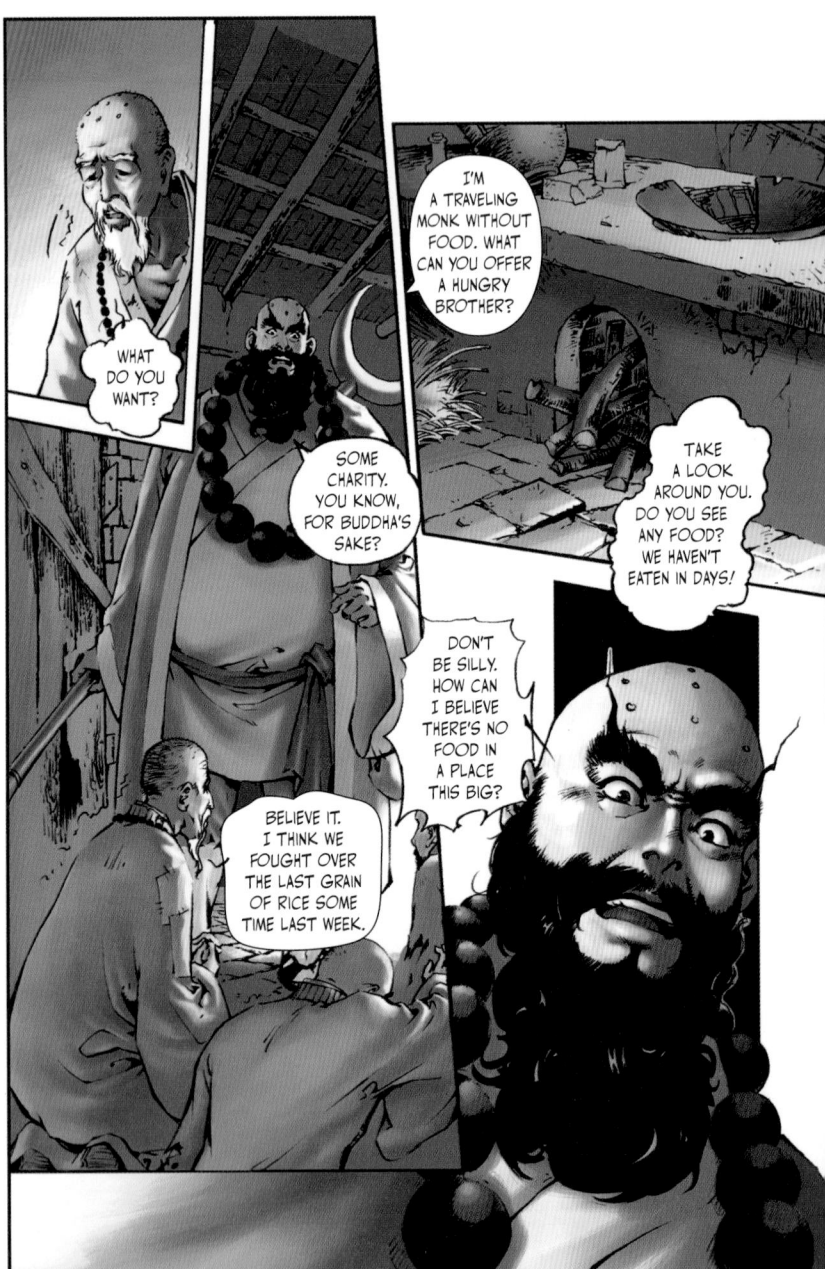

WE USED TO BE A VERY AFFLUENT TEMPLE. BUT ONE DAY WE WERE TAKEN OVER BY A VILLAINOUS MONK AND HIS SIDEKICK.

OF COURSE, IT WASN'T ALWAYS LIKE THIS AROUND HERE...

THEY NEGLECTED THE UPKEEP OF THE TEMPLE AND LET OUR GARDENS ROT. AND THEY DROVE OUT ANY PRIEST WHO CONFRONTED THEM ABOUT IT.

AND, WHAT, YOU JUST LET THEM? WHY DIDN'T YOU CONTACT THE AUTHORITIES?

THE NEAREST GOVERNMENT OFFICE IS MILES FROM HERE, AND THEY THREATENED TO BEAT US TO DEATH IF WE SET FOOT OUTSIDE THE TEMPLE.

35

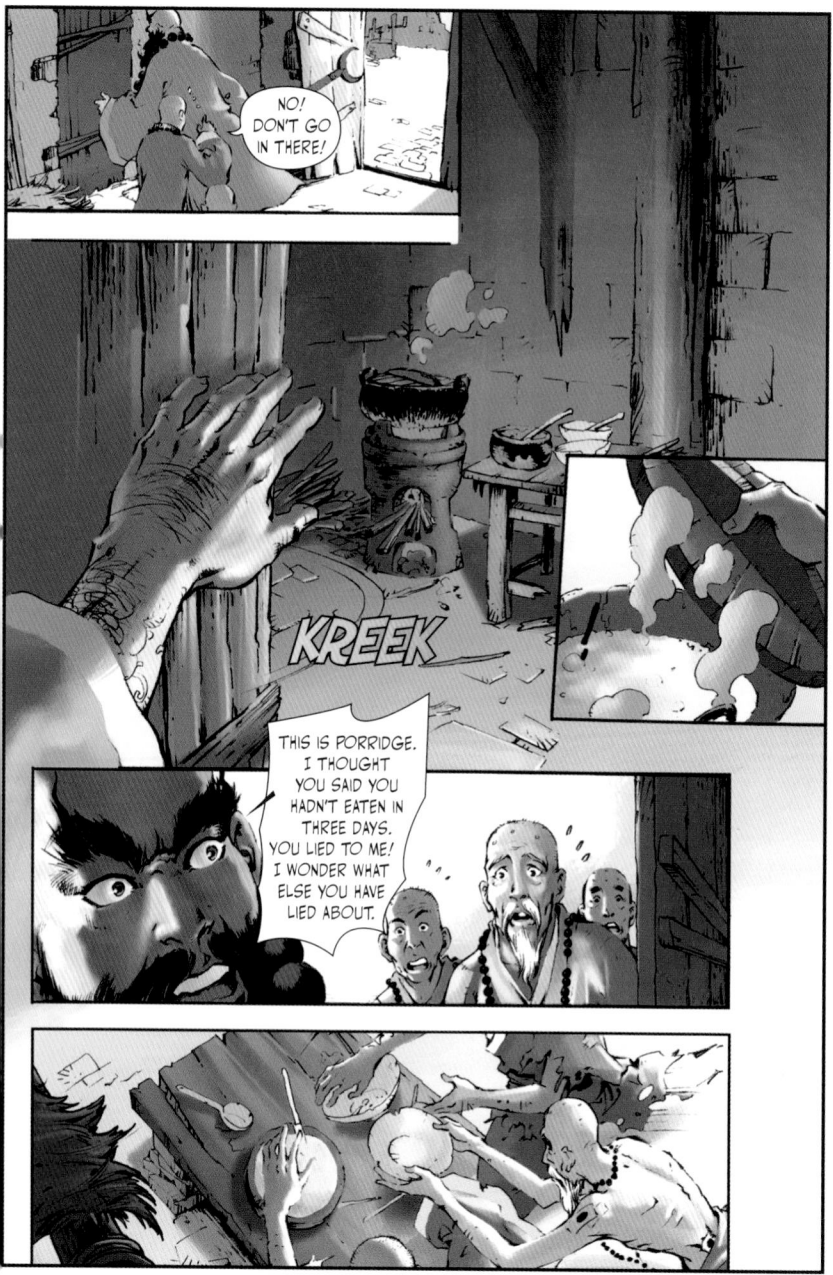

37

39

PATHETIC.

DARLING YOU HAVE NO HUSBAND; YOU'D BE LUCKY TO HAVE MEEE...

AHEM...

OKAY...THIS MAN LOOKS LIKE A MONK, BUT I CAN PRACTICALLY SMELL HIS BLOODLUST. SOMETHING ISN'T RIGHT.

ARE YOU THE FIEND WHO ALLOWED THIS TEMPLE TO FALL APART? ANSWER ME!

GOOD DAY, BROTHER. IT'S AN HONOR.

LESS FLATTERY. MORE EXPLAINING.

HERE. HAVE A SEAT. I WILL EXPLAIN THINGS.

THERE ARE A GROUP OF MONKS WHO ARE STARVING TO DEATH BECAUSE OF YOU. WHY?

YOU MISUNDERSTAND. THIS TEMPLE FELL APART BECAUSE OF THEM. THEY WERE DRUNKS AND WOMANIZERS. THAT'S WHY FLYING GIANT AND I TOOK CONTROL; TO END THE DEBAUCHERY.

45

49

53

55

I HAVE TO ADMIT: THAT STORY IS INSANE.

MY STORY IS SIMPLE BY COMPARISON. I WAS LOOKING FOR MY MASTER, AND THEN I RAN OUT OF MONEY. NOW I SPEND MY DAYS LOOKING FOR FOOD. AND TODAY WAS A GOOD DAY.

So ZhiShen sat with Jin Shi and told him how he became a monk…

I'LL BE READY IN NO TIME. YOU WOULDN'T HAVE ANY WINE, WOULD YOU?

HELP YOURSELF. WHEN YOU'RE DONE, LET'S TAKE CARE OF YOUR LITTLE MONK PROBLEM.

DongJing

I HAVE NO CHOICE BUT TO KEEP GOING TO DONGJING. TAKE CARE.

THANKS FOR THE HAND, JIN SHI. WHERE ARE YOU OFF TO NOW?

YOU TOO. UNTIL NEXT TIME, MY FRIEND.

WITH NO MONEY? NO CHOICE. I MUST RETURN TO MOUNT HUA.

FAIR ENOUGH.

EXCUSE ME. CAN EITHER OF YOU TELL ME HOW I GET TO DAXIANGUO TEMPLE?

YES. CROSS THAT BRIDGE OVER THERE...

63

Soon after, ZhiShen Lu was at the gates of the temple.

MAY I ASK WHAT YOU'RE HERE ABOUT?

I'VE BEEN SENT HERE FROM MOUNT WUTAI. I AM CARRYING A LETTER FROM ELDER ZHIZHEN.

GREETINGS, BROTHER. HOW CAN I HELP YOU?

I'M LOOKING FOR ELDER ZHIQING.

AH, ELDER ZHIZHEN! VERY WELL, PLEASE COME INSIDE.

"DEAREST BROTHER, LET ME PRESENT ZHISHEN LU. PLEASE ACCEPT HIM INTO YOUR TEMPLE. HE IS WANTED FOR MURDER, BUT HAS MUCH POTENTIAL."

BROTHER, YOU HAVE TRAVELED FAR. GO CLEAN UP, THEN WE WILL DISCUSS THIS.

THANK YOU, BROTHER.

I THINK ELDER ZHIZHEN HAS LOST HIS MIND. HOW CAN HE ASK THIS?

HE KNOWS WE CAN'T ACCEPT SOMEONE WANTED FOR MURDER.

I AGREE. BUT I AM IN NO POSITION TO TURN DOWN THE REQUEST. WE CANNOT REFUSE TO ACCEPT HIM. SO WHAT DO WE DO?

WELL, NOTHING ABOUT HIM IS MONK-LIKE, SO IT'S OBVIOUS HE CAN'T LIVE IN THE TEMPLE. BUT THEN AGAIN, HE MAY NOT HAVE TO.

I SAY WE SEND HIM TO THE FARM ON THE OUTSKIRTS OF OUR LAND. HE CAN BE THE CARETAKER, OUT OF SIGHT AND OUT OF OUR WAY.

BESIDES, WE NEED SOMEONE TO MANAGE THOSE USELESS FARMHANDS.

THAT IS A FANTASTIC SUGGESTION, BROTHER. MAKE IT SO.

65

ZhiShen had even less desire to run a farm than he had to become a monk, but he was in no place to refuse the job.

JUST SO WE'RE CLEAR, I DON'T KNOW THE FIRST THING ABOUT FARMING. I COULDN'T TELL AN OX FROM A PLOW.

YOU'LL FIGURE IT OUT. BESIDES, THIS IS ONLY UNTIL SOMETHING BETTER COMES ALONG.

IF THAT'S THE CASE...I GUESS I CAN DO IT.

The farmhands were notified that ZhiShen Lu was their new supervisor. Almost immediately, they mocked him and plotted to humiliate him.

LOOKS LIKE THEY'RE SENDING SOMEONE ELSE TO BE IN CHARGE OF US.

WHAT IS THIS, THE SIXTH PERSON? THEY'LL NEVER LEARN, WILL THEY?

A MAN WHO RUNS A FARM SHOULD KNOW THE GROUNDS. STARTING WITH THE MANURE PIT.

GOOD IDEA. WE CAN GIVE HIM A GUIDED TOUR!

OOH, I LIKE THIS PLAN.

HA HA!

MY LORD, CAN WE START OVER AGAIN? WE DID NOT MEAN TO HARM YOU IN ANY WAY. THIS TEMPLE HAS BEEN VERY GOOD TO US.

THE MONKS HAVE SHELTERED US WHEN OUR GAMBLING ENDANGERED OUR LIVES AND COST US OUR HOMES.

WE'VE BEEN WORKING THE FARM AS A WAY OF EARNING A LIVING TO PAY OFF OUR DEBTS. WE DON'T MEAN TO INTIMIDATE YOU.

INTIMIDATE ME? DID YOU KNOW I BECAME A MONK AFTER I KILLED A MAN WITH ONLY THREE BLOWS?

PRIOR TO THAT, I WAS A MILITARY MAN. I BEAT WHOLE ARMIES MYSELF.

BELIEVE ME, YOU FOOLS DON'T SCARE ME IN THE LEAST. REMEMBER THAT FROM NOW ON, YES?

YES, MY LORD. WE WILL REMEMBER.

PLOINK

YES! RIGHT AWAY.

NO, THE TREE!

ECH. SORRY, MY LORD. IT'S THAT STUPID NEST UP THERE.

WAIT. YOU WANT US TO GET RID OF THE TREE, AND NOT JUST THE NEST? HOW ARE WE SUPPOSED TO DO THAT?

NEST?

SO GET RID OF IT.

STAND ASIDE, ALL OF YOU, AND I'LL SHOW YOU HOW.

HA HA HA! WELL, I'M NO ORDINARY MAN, THAT'S FOR SURE. BUT I'M NOT EVEN A BUDDHIST, MUCH LESS A BUDDHA!

HAVE A SEAT, MY LORD.

HAVE A DRINK.

From that moment on, the farmhands never gave ZhiShen Lu an ounce of trouble. They even called him "Master."

MASTER, COULD YOU PERHAPS SHOW US YOUR MARTIAL ARTS SKILLS?

I'LL NEED SOMEONE TO FETCH MY WEAP-- AH, THERE IT IS!

OF COURSE!

81

I KNEW I RECOGNIZED YOUR NAME...

YEARS AGO, I FOUGHT ALONGSIDE YOUR FATHER, MAJOR LIN.

I'M SORRY I DIDN'T RECOGNIZE YOU SOONER. FROM NOW ON, I SHOULD LIKE TO CALL YOU BROTHER.

YES, HE SPOKE WELL OF YOU. IT'S AN HONOR TO FINALLY MEET YOU IN PERSON.

ZhiShen Lu and Chong Lin pledged an oath of fidelity on the spot, and became sworn brothers.

SO, BROTHER, WHAT BRINGS YOU TO THE TEMPLE?

THERE'S STILL PLENTY OF WINE LEFT, BROTHER. I SAY WE SIT HERE AND WORSHIP TOGETHER! HA HA!

MY WIFE AND I COME HERE OFTEN TO WORSHIP. THAT'S WHERE WE WERE HEADED WHEN I SAW YOU.

YOU DON'T NEED TO GO TO THE TEMPLE.

THIS ROUND'S ON ME!

Chapter 2

The Plight of Chong Lin

Summary

Chong Lin and ZhiShen Lu are in the middle of their reunion when Chong Lin receives word that his wife is being viciously harassed by Qiu Gao's son. Chong Lin rushes to his wife's defense, but YaNei Gao, who never fails to get his way, is undeterred. He devises a scheme by which to steal Chong Lin's wife away from him, and enlists the help of Chong Lin's childhood friend Qian Lu. When the scheme results in Chong Lin being found guilty of a crime, he only barely escapes a death sentence. Banished into exile, Chong Lin is escorted by two villainous soldiers, who are under orders to deal with him in the worst possible way. But before they can carry out their orders, an unexpected savior emerges, quite literally, from the woodwork, and Chong Lin's fate looks less than sealed.

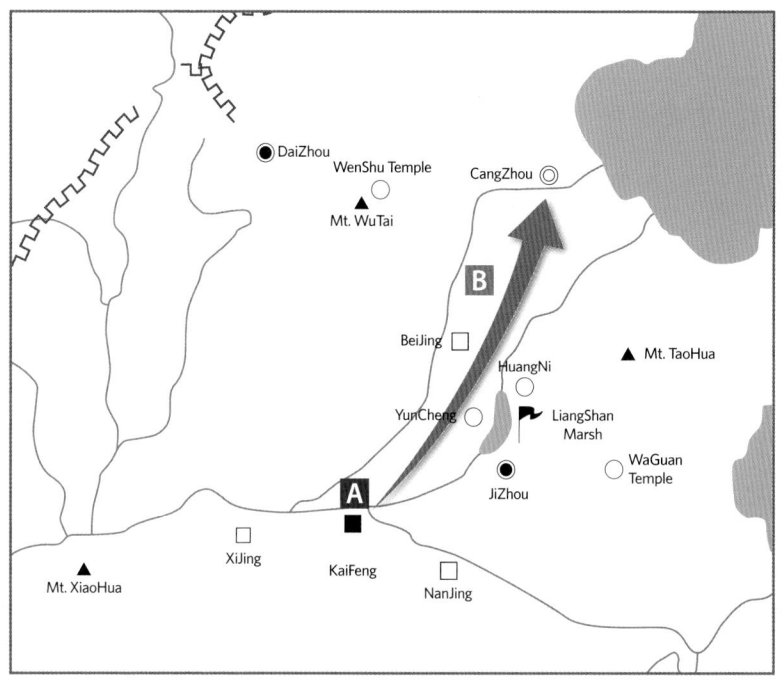

A YaNei Gao develops an obsession with Chong Lin's wife, so he sets into motion a plot to have Chong Lin executed.

B Chong Lin is spared a death sentence from the court of KaiFeng, but is banished from the kingdom and sentenced to serve exile in CangZhou.

93

Down at the temple, Chong Lin's wife was being harassed by none other than YaNei Gao, adopted son of the treacherous Qiu Gao. Qiu Gao was the most powerful man in the land, and YaNei behaved without fear of getting into trouble, because he never did.

YANEI GAO

LET ME PASS!

WHY? WE'RE HAVING FUN HERE!

YOU HAVE SOME NERVE. HOW DARE YOU?

HOW DARE I? NOW WHO'S GOT THE NERVE?

WHY SO SAD, PRETTY LADY? ALL I WANT TO DO IS TREAT YOU RIGHT.

HELLO, BROTHER.

YOU'RE SAFE NOW.

THIS IS NO TIME FOR WORDS! WHO'S GETTING A BEAT-DOWN?

RELAX, ZHISHEN. THERE'S NOTHING TO BE DONE HERE. THE OFFENDER IS THE ADOPTED SON OF QIU GAO. TO ATTACK HIM IS TO COMMIT TREASON. WE'D BE AS GOOD AS DEAD.

I DON'T GIVE A FLYING LEAP ABOUT QIU GAO. POINT THIS BRAT OUT TO ME, AND I'LL CUT HIM IN TWO!

I CAN'T. I WORK FOR QIU GAO, SO I CAN'T FIGHT HIS SON.

Despite being told that he was lusting after another man's wife, YaNei Gao couldn't help himself. He was obsessed with the woman he'd earlier harassed.

LOST IN THOUGHT, I SEE. MUST BE ABOUT CHONG LIN'S WIFE, YES?

AN FU

YES, I THOUGHT AS MUCH.

MY LORD! I'VE COME TO CHECK UP ON YOU.

NOT TO WORRY. I HAVE A PLAN.

SIGH...

OH? DOES YOUR PLAN INVOLVE MAKING CHONG LIN'S WIFE MINE?

YOU KNOW WHAT? IT ACTUALLY DOES.

QIAN LU OWES ME A FAVOR OR TWO. SO I'LL SEND HIM OVER TO CHONG LIN'S HOME, WHERE HE'LL TAKE HIS OLD FRIEND FOR A DRINK.

WHILE THAT'S GOING ON, I'LL SEND A MESSENGER TO CHONG LIN'S WIFE, BEARING THE NEWS THAT HER HUSBAND IS INJURED.

SHE WILL THEN ASK WHERE TO FIND HER HUSBAND. WE, IN TURN, WILL GIVE HER DIRECTIONS TO YOUR MANOR.

ONCE SHE'S ENTERED YOUR CHAMBERS, IT'S FINDERS, KEEPERS, YES?

CLAP CLAP

YES...YES! A FANTASTIC IDEA! BUT IT MUST BE DONE RIGHT AWAY.

I INSIST YOU SPEAK WITH QIAN LU. AS IN, NOW.

AS YOU WISH, MY LORD.

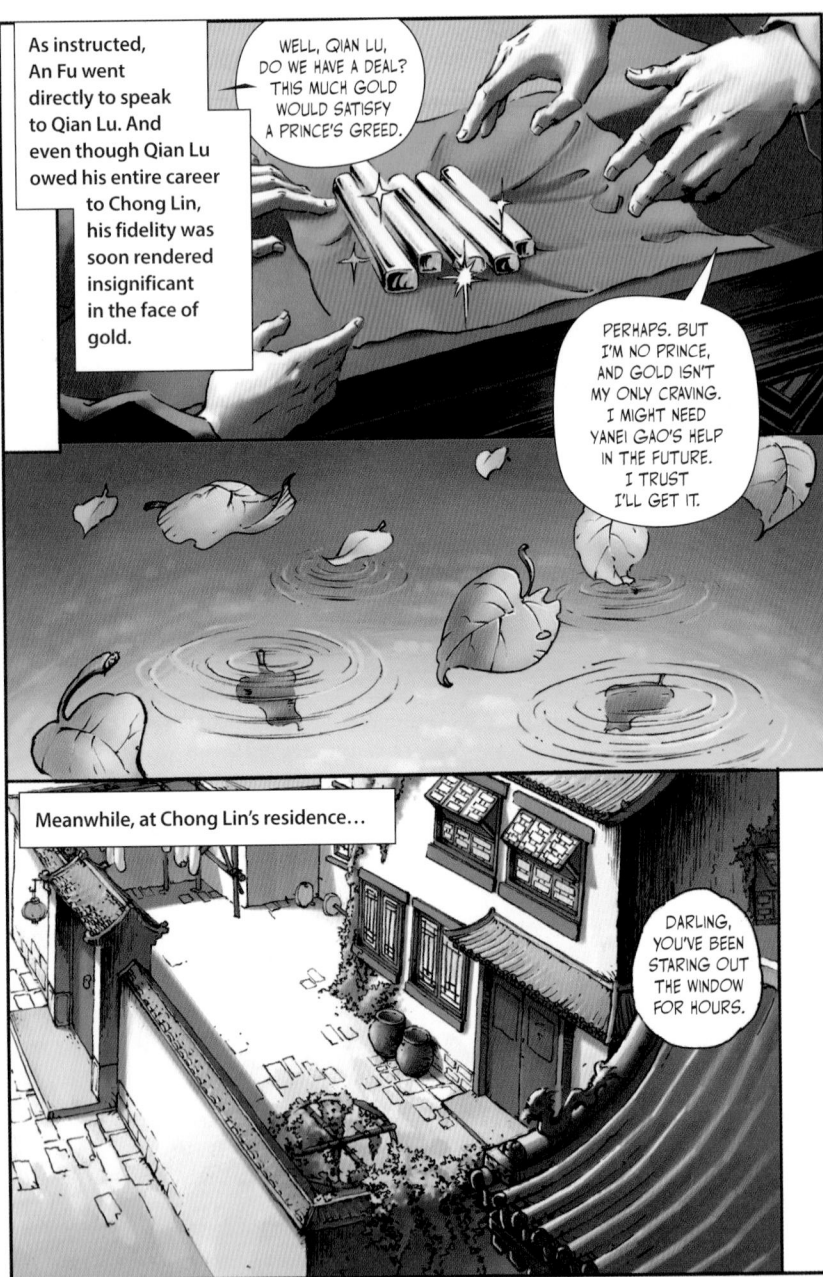

As instructed, An Fu went directly to speak to Qian Lu. And even though Qian Lu owed his entire career to Chong Lin, his fidelity was soon rendered insignificant in the face of gold.

WELL, QIAN LU, DO WE HAVE A DEAL? THIS MUCH GOLD WOULD SATISFY A PRINCE'S GREED.

PERHAPS. BUT I'M NO PRINCE, AND GOLD ISN'T MY ONLY CRAVING. I MIGHT NEED YANEI GAO'S HELP IN THE FUTURE. I TRUST I'LL GET IT.

Meanwhile, at Chong Lin's residence…

DARLING, YOU'VE BEEN STARING OUT THE WINDOW FOR HOURS.

105

HERE WE GO...HERE'S TO SUSTAINING OLD FRIENDSHIPS AND AVOIDING NEW RIVALRIES.

INDEED. CHEERS.

WHAT IS IT? WHAT'S BUGGING YOU?

PONK

WHAT'S BUGGING ME IS THAT I'M A SOLDIER. AND A GOOD MAN. I'VE EARNED WHAT I HAVE. YET I MUST ENDURE THE WHIMS OF A CHILD.

WAIT A MINUTE. YOU HAVE STARED DOWN SOLDIERS TWICE YOUR SIZE. YOU ARE ONE OF QIU GAO'S FAVORITE MARSHALS. WHY EXACTLY MUST YOU SUFFER A CHILD?

Chong Lin then told Qian Lu about his earlier encounter with YaNei Gao.

HEH HEH...

MY WORK HERE IS DONE. BEST BE ON MY WAY. THINGS ARE ABOUT TO GET QUITE UGLY HERE.

As Chong Lin was returning from the bathroom, one of his maids approached him. She was in tears.

MY LORD! MY LORD!

113

115

GLUG

BUT I REFUSE TO SIT IDLY BY AND BE INSULTED BY BOTH MAN AND FATE.

I SAID, LET ME GO! WHERE IS QIAN LU? I'M GOING TO CUT OUT THAT BASTARD'S HEART!

DARLING, PLEASE! YOU'LL ONLY ENDANGER US! I WASN'T HARMED, IN THE END. AND I'LL BE MORE CAREFUL.

YaNei Gao had injured himself jumping out of the window. But, fearing Qiu Gao's wrath, he lied about the nature of his ailment.

PLEASE, DON'T DO ANYTHING THAT WOULD TAKE YOU AWAY FROM ME! I COULDN'T BEAR IT. OH, THIS IS ALL MY FAULT.

ALL YOUR... WHAT ARE YOU TALKING ABOUT?

I FEEL LIKE DUNG.

BELIEVE ME, I KNOW WHO'S TO BLAME.

YOU NEED TO REST, MY LORD. THAT LEG WON'T HEAL ITSELF.

119

THANK YOU. WE'LL DO THE REST.

WE'LL SEE ABOUT THAT...

BEATEN AND LOVESICK? WHAT A CHUMP.

THUD

WHAT CAN I TELL YOU, MY LORD? YOUR SON THINKS HE'S DYING.

GRAND MARSHAL QIU GAO

HM...CHONG LIN IS ONE OF MY FINEST MARSHALS. BUT EVEN HE CANNOT BE ALLOWED TO ASSAULT MY SON LIKE THAT.

MY LORD, AN FU AND QIAN LU TELL ME THEY HAVE A PLAN.

FINE. GO FETCH THEM.

THANK YOU FOR SEEING US, GRAND MARSHAL.

STAND UP.

COME ON, FOLKS! YOU ARE STANDING JUST FEET AWAY FROM LEGENDARY WEAPONRY. THIS SWORD WOULD CUT DOWN A GOD!

?

DOESN'T ANYONE KNOW SWORDS?

LET ME TAKE A LOOK AT THIS.

I DO. COME HERE.

AH, FINALLY! A MAN OF TASTE. THIS BLADE IS WORTH 3,000 COINS, BUT I'LL SELL IT TO YOU FOR 2,000.

IT *IS* A RARE SWORD.

THUMP

GOOD DAY, MY LORD.

OH, NO. HE'S IN HERE.

WHO'S THERE? CHONG LIN?

WHAT ARE YOU DOING HERE? I DIDN'T SUMMON YOU.

AND WHY DID YOU BRING A SWORD TO A SACRED SHRINE? TO KILL ME? TO EVEN THREATEN ME IS AN ACT OF TREASON!

NO!!!!

TAKE HIM INTO CUSTODY AND HAVE HIM STAND BEFORE KAIFENG COURT!

THIS IS JUST A MISTAKE! MY LORD!

GRAND MARSHAL, PLEASE BELIEVE ME!

YIN FU, YOU HAVE TO BELIEVE ME!

I'M INNOCENT!

Chong Lin was taken to KaiFeng Court, where he was almost immediately put on trial.

SILENCE, TRAITOR!

The trial was rigged, though, as Qiu Gao had already sent one of his men to Yin Fu, with instructions to have Chong Lin put to death.

YOU ADMIT YOU ENTERED BAIHU SHRINE WITH A SWORD?

THAT ALONE IS A GRAVE OFFENSE. BUT TO THREATEN GRAND MARSHAL GAO IS A CAPITAL OFFENSE!

MY LORD, I AM A MARSHAL OF THE IMPERIAL GUARD. I HAVE BEEN IN THE MILITARY MOST OF MY LIFE. I HAVE SERVED WITH HONOR AND FIDELITY. IF ANYONE KNOWS THE LAW, IT'S ME.

SO BELIEVE ME WHEN I SAY I AM TELLING THE TRUTH: QIU GAO'S SON HAS HIS EYE ON MY WIFE. A FEW DAYS AGO, HE STARTED HARASSING HER. IN FRONT OF A TEMPLE, NO LESS.

SOON AFTER, MY CHILDHOOD FRIEND VISITED ME AND TOOK ME OUT FOR A DRINK. DURING THIS TIME, YANEI GAO MADE ANOTHER ATTEMPT AT MY WIFE, TRYING TO STEAL HER AWAY.

TODAY, I WAS TOLD GRAND MARSHAL GAO WANTED TO SEE MY NEW SWORD. I WAS SUMMONED TO BAIHU TEMPLE, AND I ENTERED NOT REALIZING WHAT IT WAS. I NEVER WOULD HAVE ENTERED WITH A WEAPON IF I WASN'T ORDERED!

I UNDERSTAND I BROKE THE LAW. BUT I NEED YOU TO UNDERSTAND THAT I BELIEVE I'VE BEEN SET UP. I BELIEVE YANEI GAO WANTS ME OUT OF THE WAY SO HE CAN HAVE MY WIFE.

THIS IS THE TRUTH. I SWEAR TO THE HEAVENS.

HM...

131

Yin Fu was faced a predicament. The details of Chong Lin's story made sense, but KaiFeng Court was in no position to act against the will of Qiu Gao.

The deliberations would be tense.

TAKE HIM AWAY WHILE WE DECIDE.

Yin Fu couldn't make up his mind during the deliberations. So it fell to another official, Ding Sun, to speak some sense to the court.

Of course, to convince Yin Fu that he was right, Ding Sun would have to appeal to his vanity.

MY FRIENDS, CHONG LIN HAS SERVED THIS COUNTRY WITH DISTINCTION FOR MANY YEARS. I CAN'T BELIEVE HE'D WILLINGLY BREAK THE LAW.

AND WE ALL KNOW ABOUT YANEI GAO. I BELIEVE CHONG LIN'S STORY.

MIND YOUR TONGUE, DING SUN!

BUT THE GRAND MARSHAL GAVE ORDERS!

THIS COURT DOES NOT BELONG TO HIM. HE'S NOT IN CHARGE HERE!

I'M ONLY ASKING FOR A FEW MINUTES.

Marshal Zhang, Chong Lin's father-in-law, met the exile party at the gates of the city. Together, they went to a local tavern.

HOW ARE YOU HOLDING UP?

PLEASE. LET ME HAVE ONE LAST DRINK WITH MY SON-IN-LAW.

I'M FINE. I WAS BEATEN, BUT I CAN WALK WITHOUT PAIN.

THAT'S GOOD. NOW LISTEN TO ME: YOU NEED TO KEEP YOUR HEAD DOWN, KEEP YOUR MIND FOCUSED ON CARRYING OUT YOUR SENTENCE WITH LITTLE FUSS.

FATHER, THERE'S NO GUARANTEE THAT I WILL BE COMING BACK. I'M NOT SURE THEY WON'T JUST KILL ME ONCE WE'RE FAR ENOUGH AWAY.

WHATEVER HAPPENS, SHE MUST FIND HAPPINESS AGAIN. YOU MUST LET HER REMARRY.

AND AS MUCH AS IT BREAKS MY HEART TO SAY IT, YOU MUST FIND HER A NEW HUSBAND IMMEDIATELY. OTHERWISE, YANEI GAO WILL CLAIM HER FOR HIS OWN.

I'LL BRING MY [DA]UGHTER HOME TO [LI]VE WITH ME WHILE [YO]U'RE AWAY. THEN, [W]HEN YOU RETURN, [T]HE TWO OF YOU [C]AN BE REUNITED.

135

137

KLANK

KLANK

HURRY IT UP, MAGGOT! I'D LIKE TO GET THERE DURING THIS LIFETIME!

I CAN'T WALK ANY FASTER THAN THIS. MY FEET ARE NOTHING BUT BLISTERS.

What Chong Lin didn't know was that his two escorts were bribed by Qian Lu, who had given them special instructions…

I DON'T WANT EXCUSES! MOVE IT!

143

SPLOCK

GAH!!!

WHAT ARE YOU DOING?!

IT BURNS!

WHAT'S GOING ON?

I TRIED TO WASH HIS FEET.

HE DIDN'T LIKE IT. FINE. BED, THEN.

SO...

SO MUCH PAIN...

LET'S REST IN THE WOODS OVER THERE.

FINE BY ME. I NEED THE SHADE.

DESPITE THE EXCITEMENT, THERE WAS SOMETHING OMINOUS ABOUT THE WOODS.

IT'S SO NICE HERE!

153

159

SAVE IT!
ONCE A LIAR,
ALWAYS A LIAR.

NO, MY LORD!
I SWEAR,
THAT'S NOT WHAT
I MEANT!

AHH...

≩ BRRRRRP ≩
WHOO.
I'M STUFFED.

ALL RIGHT.
ON WE GO.

PLINK

IT'S TIME TO PART WAYS, ZHISHEN. YOU DON'T NEED TO COME ALONG ANY FARTHER.

THE HELL I DON'T. IF THESE TWO DON'T DO QIU GAO'S BIDDING, THEY'RE DEAD. IF THEY DO, YOU'RE DEAD. SO I STAY UNTIL CANGZHOU.

HE'S GOT A POINT. WHAT ARE WE GOING TO DO?

GAH!

HA HA!

WOW, I'VE NEVER SEEN SOMEONE TREAT SOLDIERS THE WAY THEY'RE ALWAYS TREATING US. THIS IS SO COOL!

NO KIDDING! I WANNA TRY THAT.

HERE. TAKE THESE.

YOU TWO WILL WATCH OUT FOR CHONG LIN. OR YOU'RE DEAD.

DON'T BE SO PROUD. THERE'S NOTHING TO BE ASHAMED OF.

Y--YES, OF COURSE! WE'LL TAKE GOOD CARE OF HIM.

Honor Among Outlaws

Honor is a complicated thing in a land as turbulent as China during the Song Dynasty. At a time when it is impossible to trust the motives of those who are responsible for upholding law and order, a civic code of honor between citizens that is implemented and adequately enforced by government is nonexistent. That leaves individuals to live by an honor code of their own making, and for the bandits who run from or ignore the law, it means living a contradiction: Trust only among your kind, and never trust an outlaw.

Evidence of this contradiction is visible when ZhiShen Lu steals from the two bandits who shelter him for a time. ZhiShen is on the run, having unintentionally killed a man. When he meets an old acquaintance who is also living outside the law, the two men are gracious toward each other in a way that would suggest a mutual trust. But we soon learn there are limits to a thief's honor: one day, ZhiShen's friend, Zhong Li, goes off to rob a traveling caravan and promises to give ZhiShen some of the loot to pay for his expenses. ZhiShen sees no need to profit off of a stranger being robbed, so he steals Zhong Li's finest possessions and flees.

In fact, ZhiShen embodies the contradiction of an outlaw's

life. Notice how little respect he has for the personal property of a man he knows to be a thief, or how little he seems to care that he killed a man in cold blood. Both of these men operate outside the law, but more important, they both violate some part of ZhiShen's moral code – a code he himself does not live up to. Therefore ZhiShen does not feel the need to respect fellow outlaws, even though he himself is an outlaw. Instead, ZhiShen Lu goes out of his way to help those who are victims, either of a law or at the hand of an outlaw. ZhiShen is a walking contradiction, because even though he doesn't seem to respect the law, he does not hesitate to assist those who are oppressed by it. As a result, ZhiShen embodies the central theme of *Outlaws of the Marsh:* that a man can be a hero one moment, and a tyrant the next, because there is no objective consistency to an individual's idea of right and wrong.

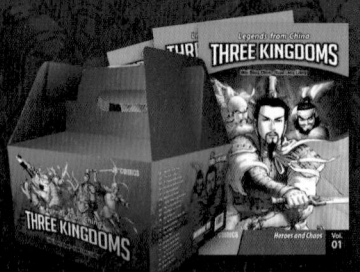

TALES FROM CHINA OUTLAWS of the MARSH

Vol. 01

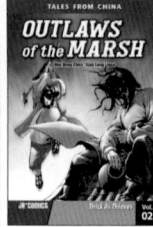
Vol. 02

Vol. 03

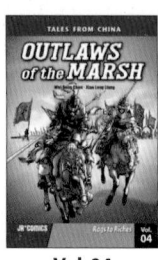
Vol. 04

Vol. 05

Vol. 06

Vol. 07

Vol. 08

Vol. 09

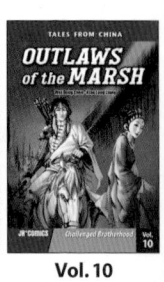
Vol. 10

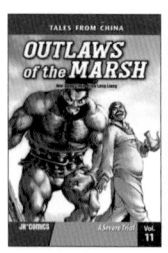
Vol. 11

Vol. 12

Vol. 13

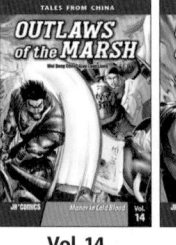
Vol. 14

Vol. 15

Vol. 16

Vol. 17

Vol. 18

Vol. 19

Vol. 20